The Sleeping Beauty

First published in 2005 by
Franklin Watts
96 Leonard Street
London
EC2A 4XD

Franklin Watts Australia
45–51 Huntley Street
Alexandria
NSW 2015

A CIP catalogue record for this book is available
from the British Library.

ISBN 0 7496 6148 8 (hbk)
ISBN 0 7496 6160 7 (pbk)

Series Editor: Jackie Hamley
Series Advisor: Dr Barrie Wade
Series Designer: Peter Scoulding

Printed in China

Another book for Daniel – love M.N.

The Sleeping Beauty

Retold by Margaret Nash

Illustrated by Barbara Vagnozzi

FRANKLIN WATTS
LONDON•SYDNEY

Once upon a time a beautiful princess was born.

The happy King and
Queen gave a feast.

They invited all the good
fairies in the land.

Each fairy gave the princess
a gift: beauty, kindness and
all good things.

The last fairy was just
waiting to give her gift …

.... when a wicked fairy
flew in. "So you didn't
invite me!" she snarled.

"Well, when that baby is
fifteen she will prick her
finger on a spindle and die!"

"I cannot break the spell, but I can make it better," said the good fairy.

"The princess will not die, but she will sleep for a hundred years."

The King and Queen
burned all the spindles
in the land.

Fifteen years passed.

On her fifteenth birthday,
the princess climbed up a
tower she had never
visited before.

Inside, an old lady was spinning. "Please, let me try," said the princess.

She picked up the spindle.
"OW!" she cried. She'd
pricked her finger!

The princess fell asleep.

Everyone else in the castle fell asleep, too!

21

Years passed by. A thorn
hedge grew up around
the castle. Nobody
could get through.

After a hundred years, a prince came to the castle. The thorns parted.

The prince got into the courtyard ...

... through the hall ...

.... and up to the tower.

There he found the
beautiful sleeping princess.
He woke her with a kiss.

Everyone else woke up, too!

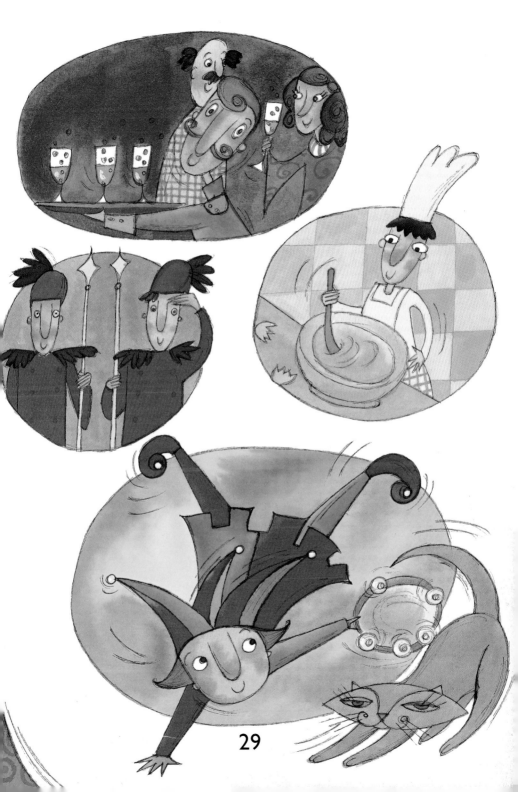

29

The prince married the beautiful princess.

And they lived happily
ever after.

31

Leapfrog has been specially designed to fit the requirements of the National Literacy Strategy. It offers real books for beginning readers by top authors and illustrators.

There are 31 Leapfrog stories to choose from:

The Bossy Cockerel
Written by Margaret Nash, illustrated by Elisabeth Moseng

Bill's Baggy Trousers
Written by Susan Gates, illustrated by Anni Axworthy

Mr Spotty's Potty
Written by Hilary Robinson, illustrated by Peter Utton

Little Joe's Big Race
Written by Andy Blackford, illustrated by Tim Archbold

The Little Star
Written by Deborah Nash, illustrated by Richard Morgan

The Cheeky Monkey
Written by Anne Cassidy, illustrated by Lisa Smith

Selfish Sophie
Written by Damian Kelleher, illustrated by Georgie Birkett

Recycled!
Written by Jillian Powell, illustrated by Amanda Wood

Felix on the Move
Written by Maeve Friel, illustrated by Beccy Blake

Pippa and Poppa
Written by Anne Cassidy, illustrated by Philip Norman

Jack's Party
Written by Ann Bryant, illustrated by Claire Henley

The Best Snowman
Written by Margaret Nash, illustrated by Jörg Saupe

Eight Enormous Elephants
Written by Penny Dolan, illustrated by Leo Broadley

Mary and the Fairy
Written by Penny Dolan, illustrated by Deborah Allwright

The Crying Princess
Written by Anne Cassidy, illustrated by Colin Paine

Jasper and Jess
Written by Anne Cassidy, illustrated by François Hall

The Lazy Scarecrow
Written by Jillian Powell, illustrated by Jayne Coughlin

The Naughty Puppy
Written by Jillian Powell, illustrated by Summer Durantz

Freddie's Fears
Written by Hilary Robinson, illustrated by Ross Collins

Cinderella
Written by Barrie Wade, illustrated by Julie Monks

The Three Little Pigs
Written by Maggie Moore, illustrated by Rob Hefferan

Jack and the Beanstalk
Written by Maggie Moore, illustrated by Steve Cox

The Three Billy Goats Gruff
Written by Barrie Wade, illustrated by Nicola Evans

Goldilocks and the Three Bears
Written by Barrie Wade, illustrated by Kristina Stephenson

Little Red Riding Hood
Written by Maggie Moore, illustrated by Paula Knight

Rapunzel
Written by Hilary Robinson, illustrated by Martin Impey

Snow White
Written by Anne Cassidy, illustrated by Melanie Sharp

The Emperor's New Clothes
Written by Karen Wallace, illustrated by François Hall

The Pied Piper of Hamelin
Written by Anne Adeney, illustrated by Jan Lewis

Hansel and Gretel
Written by Penny Dolan, illustrated by Graham Philpot

The Sleeping Beauty
Written by Margaret Nash, illustrated by Barbara Vagnozzi